A NOTE TO PARENTS

ongratulations on choosing the best in educational materials r your child. By selecting top-quality McGraw-Hill products, ou can be assured that the concepts used in our books will inforce and enhance the skills that are being taught in assrooms nationwide.

nd what better way to get young readers excited than with ercer Mayer's Little Critter, a character loved by children erywhere? Our First Readers offer simple and engaging ories about Little Critter that children can read on their own. ach level incorporates reading skills, colorful illustrations, nd challenging activities.

evel 1 – The stories are simple and use repetitive language. ustrations are highly supportive.
evel 2 - The stories begin to grow in complexity. Language is ill repetitive, but it is mixed with more challenging ocabulary.
evel 3 - The stories are more complex. Sentences are longer nd more varied.

o help your child make the most of this book, look at the first w pictures in the story and discuss what is happening. Ask our child to predict where the story is going. Then, once your iild has read the story, have him or her review the word list nd do the activities. This will reinforce vocabulary words om the story and build reading comprehension.

ou are your child's first and most influential teacher. No one lows your child the way you do. Tailor your time together to inforce a newly acquired skill or to overcome a temporary umbling block. Praise your child's progress and ideas, take elight in his or her imagination, and most of all, enjoy your me together!

This product has been aligned to state and national organization standards usin
the Align to Achieve Standards Database. Align to Achieve, Inc., is an indepen-
dent, not-for-profit organization that facilitates the evaluation and improvemen
of academic standards and student achievement. To find how this product align*
to your standards, go to www.MHstandards.com.

 **Children's Publishing**

Send all inquiries to:
McGraw-Hill Children's Publishing
8787 Orion Place
Columbus, OH 43240-4027

Printed in the United States of America.

1-57768-578-4

 A Big Tuna Trading Company, LLC/J. R. Sansevere Book

Library of Congress Cataloging-in-Publication Data is on file with the publisher.

1 2 3 4 5 6 7 8 9 10 PHXBK 08 07 06 05 04 03

FIRST READERS

Level **3**   Grades **1–2**

HARVEST
TIME

by Mercer Mayer

 **Children's Publishing**

Columbus, Ohio

It's harvest time at Grandma and Grandpa's farm. Grandpa says there's a lot to be done!

First, we go to the pumpkin patch.
Grandpa shows us how to clip the
pumpkins from the vines.
"Look, Grandpa!" I hold up a great
big pumpkin for him to see.

We load the trailer full of pumpkins.
Grandpa lets us pick out some
pumpkins to take home.

Now, it's time to pick apples. We climb the ladder so we can reach the branches. We pile the apples in baskets. "Did you taste an apple, Little Critter?" calls Grandpa.
I take a big bite. It's crunchy and sour!

Next, we go for a hayride. Grandpa drives the tractor. Little Sister and I ride on the hay bales in the trailer. Our ride ends at the barn. We stack the bales of hay inside.

10

Now, we have lots of hay for the cows to eat over the winter," says Grandpa.

Then, we help Grandpa do some more chores.

We take down the scarecrow.

We fix the broken fence in the meadow.

Last, we wash all the garden tools so that they'll be clean for the spring.

13

Now, it's time for some fun!" calls Grandma.
We go inside to help make apple pies. Grandma lets me measure the flour and the sugar. Little Sister rolls the dough. I can't wait until the pies are ready!

Before dinner, Grandma makes hot apple cider with cinnamon. Then, we have a big meal, with apple pie and vanilla ice cream for dessert.

"Thanks for all your hard work!" says Grandpa. "Harvest time is a busy time at the farm."

"I don't mind the hard work," I say, "as long as there's apple pie for dessert!"

"And ice cream, too!" says Little Sister.

17

Word List

Read each word in the lists below. Then, find each word in the story. Now, make up a new sentence using the word. Say your sentence out loud.

Words I Know
apple
barn
inside
pie
pumpkin
time
winter

Challenge Words
chores
climb
crunchy
dessert
harvest
hayride
measure

Easy as Pie

t the end of the story, Little Critter and Little
ister helped Grandma make apple pies. Point
o the pictures of things they used to make the
ies.

Sequencing

Look at the pictures below. Then, point to the pictures in the order that they happened in the story. Read the story again if you need help.

Rhyming Words

The words cat and mat are rhyming words.
Point to a word in the column on the left.
Then, point to the word that rhymes with
it in the column on the right.

chore   fool

ow   grow

ool   tie

un   more

pie   bun

dough   now

Long I Words

Long i is the sound found in the words mine and kite. Look at the lists below. Point to the words that have the long i sound.

time   cute

farm   pie

vine   nose

climb   bake

harvest   plate

pick   kite

Now, think of your own long i words. Can yo think of 5 new words?

22

Vocabulary Quiz

Answer each of the questions below. The answers should have the same number of letters as the dashed lines.

What time of year is it at the farm?

— — — — — — —

What did Little Critter and Little Sister put in the trailer?

— — — — — — — —

Little Critter's apple tasted crunchy and _____.

— — — —

What did Little Critter and Little Sister help Grandpa fix?

— — — — —

What did Little Critter and Little Sister help Grandma bake?

23

— — — — — — — —

Answer Key

page 19
Easy as Pie

apple

flour

sugar

oven

bowl

page 20
Sequencing

1

2

3

4

page 21
Rhyming Words

chore **and** more

cow **and** now

tool **and** fool

fun **and** bun

pie **and** tie

dough **and** grow

page 22
Long I Words

time
vine
climb
pie
kite

hayride
drive
ride
inside
cider
Other answers will vary.

page 23
Vocabulary Quiz

harvest

pumpkins

sour

fence

apple pies